For Alber
NC

For my cubs, Rose and Nina
CL

Text copyright © 2024 by Nick Crumpton
Illustrations copyright © 2024 by Colleen Larmour

All rights reserved. No part of this book may be reproduced, transmitted, or stored in an information retrieval system in any form or by any means, graphic, electronic, or mechanical, including photocopying, taping, and recording, without prior written permission from the publisher.

First US edition 2024
First published by Walker Books Ltd. (UK) 2024
Library of Congress Catalog Card Number pending
ISBN 978-1-5362-3877-8

24 25 26 27 28 29 CCP 10 9 8 7 6 5 4 3 2 1

Printed in Shenzhen, Guangdong, China

This book was typeset in Avenir.
The illustrations were done in mixed media.

Candlewick Press
99 Dover Street
Somerville, Massachusetts 02144

www.candlewick.com

BROWN BEARS

Dr. Nick Crumpton

illustrated by
Colleen Larmour

CANDLEWICK PRESS

Through a carpet of pine needles and a small hill of moss, twigs, and soil, three shiny black noses push up into the crisp air. Spring has arrived in Alaska.

This brown bear was alone when she fell asleep at the start of winter. Now she is climbing out of her den with two new cubs—one male and one female. They were born in February, just a few weeks ago, and have never seen the sky.

Female brown bears give birth to their tiny cubs in their dens while they are hibernating. The cubs are born blind and almost hairless. Their mother shares her body warmth and feeds them her thick, fatty milk.

The cubs' mother teaches them how to survive in the wilderness. By watching and copying her, they learn how to use their long claws to climb trees like the clean-smelling lodgepole pine . . .

how to leave their scent behind to let other bears know they were there . . .

and how to scratch bugs off their skin by dancing against trees.

Although all this might look like fun for the young bears, these activities are very important. They help the cubs' muscles grow stronger and teach them skills that will help them protect themselves later in life.

Sometimes the bears' noses lead them toward the wonderful-smelling food that people have thrown away. It's hard to stay away from these smells, but it's dangerous to stay here for long. This used to be the bears' land, but now people don't want them near their homes.

Brown bears have a better sense of smell than both dogs and cats. Some smells, like licorice, peanut butter, and even toothpaste, are irresistible to bears and can attract them to places like campsites.

When they stray close to where humans live, it can be dangerous for the people and the bears. They will both try to defend themselves from what frightens them.

After six months, the leaves on the trees begin to turn red and orange, and the meadows and forests become full of edible treats. The bears pick sweet, fat buffalo berries and huckleberries straight off the bush with their soft, sensitive lips and feast on shiny pine nuts, fallen from the trees above. No matter how much they eat, the bears never seem to feel full.

In the fall, adult brown bears can eat around 90 pounds (40 kilograms) of food in one day to prepare for hibernation. That's the same weight as an average twelve-year-old child! This gives the bears a huge layer of fat more than 4 inches (10 centimeters) thick under their skin. These fat reserves protect the bears from the cold and give them energy in the winter when they won't be able to eat.

Brown bears hibernate every winter but hardly ever use the same den twice, preferring to build a new hollow each year. Cubs hibernate with their mothers twice: once when they are born and again a year later.

When the snow starts to fall, the cubs' mother builds a den again. She finds a good spot on the side of a hill, under the roots of a great whitebark pine tree. For three days she scrapes out the hollow.

    She builds them all spongy beds of spruce branches at the end of the tunnel and pushes her cubs safely inside. The snow will cover the entrance, trapping their warmth in the den.

They soon fall asleep, waiting for the snow to melt and the year to start again.

The winter passes as they slumber.

When brown bears are hibernating, their hearts thump only eight times per minute.
They won't eat, drink, pee, or poop the entire time they are in their den.

Finally, the cubs begin to wake as their mother stirs, rustling the spruce, dry grasses, and dusty leaves. Slowly but powerfully, she moves the earth aside and lets the fresh spring air into the den. The light hurts their eyes. It has been seven months since they have seen the sun.

It feels amazing to be outside again. The cubs tumble in the last of the snow and play around their mother. It's still cold, but their thick fur keeps them warm.

The bears look so much skinnier than when they all went underground. They can smell food—animals that didn't survive the winter—and begin to fill their empty stomachs.

While they were hibernating, the bears used up all the body fat they had put on in the fall. But now that their fat reserves have run out, they have lost up to half their weight.

Later, in the summer, thousands of salmon arrive to lay their eggs in Alaska's rocky rivers. With a bit of practice, the cubs learn how to catch them. One cub snaps at them underwater, and her mother lies across the stream so that the fish swim into her paws. There are way too many for them to eat!

After a few weeks, there are fewer salmon for the bears to find. Sometimes the cubs splash a little too far away and their mother calls them back by chomping her teeth together. She wants the cubs to stay close because she knows there are some things that even bears are scared of.

Salmon and other fish, like trout, provide the bears with lots of energy and are some of their favorite foods. When large groups of salmon swim upstream to lay their eggs, a bear can eat more than ten fish in a single afternoon.

And this is one of them.
Another bear.
A male brown bear.
He is enormous,
and he is hungry.

Male brown bears wander the landscape alone. Taller than humans when standing on two legs, they are aggressive and sometimes try to eat young bears.

Bears like to give each other space, but rarely, big meals can attract many bears to the same place at the same time.

The cubs pull themselves up a tree to try to find safety. Their mother stands between them and the stranger. He is much bigger than she is, but she will not let him hurt her cubs.

She stands up on her back feet to make herself look as large as she can. She growls and roars, letting him know she will fight fiercely with her teeth and claws to protect her cubs.

The male is frightened, and he knows he cannot get around her. The cubs watch as he stomps away. She has saved them.

A bear's jaws are extremely powerful, which means they can chew through almost anything, from soft fish to hard nuts. They can also be used to protect cubs.

Female cubs may stay with their mother longer than male cubs do. After all her cubs leave, the mother can become pregnant again, starting a new family.

Soon the air will start to cool again, the leaves will fall, and the male cub will leave his family to find a new home. But until then, the cubs will stay together, sharing and growing, playing and learning, their mother protecting them, keeping them safe. Teaching them how to be bears.

A NOTE FROM THE AUTHOR

The family of bears in this story live in Alaska, on the northwestern tip of North America. In this part of the world, brown bears are also known as **grizzly bears**, although some brown bears that live in particular places have other, special names, like the **Kodiak bears** of the Kodiak Archipelago—the largest brown bears on Earth.

Because brown bears aren't picky about their diet, they are able to live in many different environments in many countries, surviving by eating everything from nuts and berries to fish and other mammals. They are found across a huge expanse of the Northern Hemisphere, from the Alaskan tundra down to arid California and also across Europe and Asia. The **Cantabrian brown bears** live in the mountains of northern Spain, while the **Ussuri brown bears** pad through the forests of Hokkaido, Japan.

Brown Bear Range

Although brown bears are found across so much of the world, many of them are in trouble. The **Gobi brown bear** is now considered critically endangered in its Mongolian desert home, while the light-colored **Himalayan brown bear** is also extremely rare. For all their majesty and strength, brown bears are like all the other animals we share the planet with: they won't survive if their homes are taken away from them or if too many are hunted for sport by humans.

FIND OUT MORE

If you'd like to discover more about brown bears (as well as other types of bears found in other parts of the world) and find links to lots of conservation societies that help protect them, visit the **International Association for Bear Research and Management**: bearbiology.org.

INDEX

Look up the pages to find out about all these bear things.
Don't forget to look at both kinds of words: this kind and *this kind*.

cubs … **2–3, 4–5, 17, 21**

den … **10, 11, 12, 13**

fat reserves … **8, 15**

food … **7, 8, 15, 16, 17, 19**

hibernation … **3, 8, 10–13**

humans … **7**

male bears … **18–21, 23**

smell … **5, 7**